At **THE DAVID BECKHAM ACADEMY** every day is a footballing adventure. Boys and girls come along to learn about the sport, develop their skills and have fun. But it's not just about tricks and flicks . . . As David Beckham knows, the real secret behind being a Premier League player is understanding the importance of dedication, teamwork, passion and having belief in yourself. In these pages you can meet football-mad children and follow them as they live out their dreams at The Academy.

SO STEP INSIDE AND JOIN THE FUN!

Want to know what some of our readers thought of this book?

'I liked that Kate does well'

Jude, age 7

'I'd give this book 12 out of 10
because it was really good!'

Ryan, age 7

'My favourite bit was when Tom
got the Predator boots'

Jordan, age 10

'My favourite chapter was *Goal Fest*'

Joseph, age 9

'I enjoyed this story because Tom learns
how to be a team player'
Jake, age 8

'The best part of the story was at the
beginning when Tom got the surprise
of going to The Academy'
Stephen, age 10

'I like Kate the best and I like it when
she gave Tom her boots'
Stanley, age 6

'I liked the end when Kate
and Tom made friends'
Jonah, age 6

EGMONT

We bring stories to life

First published in Great Britain 2009
by Egmont UK Limited
239 Kensington High Street, London W8 6SA

Text by Matt Crossick
Cover and inside illustrations by Adam Relf
Cover photography by Anthony Mandler
Design by Becky Chilcott

ISBN 978 1 4052 4527 2

1 3 5 7 9 10 8 6 4 2

A CIP catalogue record for this title is available
from the British Library

Typeset by Avon DataSet Ltd, Bidford on Avon, Warwickshire
Printed and bound in Great Britain by the CPI Group

THE DAVID BECKHAM
ACADEMY

BOSSY BOOTS

EGMONT

CONTENTS

SHOPPING SPREE

Tom dragged his feet across the driveway at a snail's pace. His mum and gran were already sitting in the car.

'Hurry up, Tom!' called his mum out of the window. 'We've got a *lot* of shopping to do!'

'Great,' groaned Tom. 'Lots of shopping. Remind me why I have to come again?'

Tom's gran giggled. 'We need a handsome young man to tell us which clothes suit us!'

'But I'm meant to be playing football

in the park,' he complained, climbing into the back seat. 'It's not fair!'

Tom lived with three girls – his mum, his big sister and his grandma. And the worst thing about it was being dragged on long, boring shopping trips all the time.

'You've played football every waking moment for the last nine days!' said his mum as they pulled away. 'A day off won't hurt you.'

'I bet David Beckham never had to put up with this kind of thing!' he moaned. 'How do you expect me to play for England one day when I have to spend my Saturdays looking at shoes or hats or . . . whatever you're going shopping for today?'

'Well, you'll just have to ask him when you're a famous footballer yourself,' laughed Tom's mum. 'Now, first stop is going to be the jewellery shops. I want to find a nice pair of earrings to . . .'

Tom tuned out his mum's voice and stared out of the window. It was physically impossible to listen to a conversation this boring. He imagined his mates must be picking teams right now. Whichever one he was on, he knew he'd be the star striker!

'Then, after four or five hours,' his gran was saying, 'we can move on to handbag shops . . .'

Tom let out another sigh. He was even wearing his football kit, complete with boots, ready to go and play. And now he had an entire day of standing outside changing rooms to look forward to.

'And then of course some shoe shops!'

said his mum. Tom couldn't believe she actually looked excited at the thought of going to a shoe shop.

Their car pulled up at some traffic lights, and Tom looked out at the huge advertising billboard by the side of the road. It showed a famous footballer doing a dramatic overhead kick in a pair of dazzling football boots.

'Wow!' sighed Tom, gazing longingly at the poster. The boots were silver with special 'blade' studs. They looked a bit like something from outer space.

'And then in the second shoe shop, I want to . . .' droned Tom's mum.

Tom looked down at the mucky, frayed bits of leather on his feet. The stitching was coming away on the toes and the right boot had sticky tape wrapped round a hole in the heel.

'Mum, will any of the shoe shops sell football boots?' he interrupted.

His mum turned round with a frown. 'I'm not made of money, love.'

Tom's eyes widened. She could have fooled him with all this talk of jewellery and bags and shoes. It seemed she had read his mind.

'Sorry, darling. But the way you're growing they wouldn't last five minutes. Your gran and I are as big as we'll ever be. I hope!' she said, laughing at her own joke.

Tom rolled his eyes. There was *no way* he could put up with 8 hours of this. He pressed his nose against the car window – he liked this bit of the journey to town: they were driving past the back of The David Beckham Academy.

'Mum, one day, can I . . .' he began, but he didn't even finish his sentence. It wasn't even worth asking for a trip to The Academy, he decided. Not until nearer his birthday, and that was 10 months away!

'And then we can stop for a cup of tea, before looking at hats,' his gran was saying. He imagined the big pitches inside The Academy's arches, full of teams learning new skills and playing in great tournaments. And here he was, spending a day looking at hats. His mum turned the car off the main road and into a huge car park.

'*Muuum!*' Tom groaned. 'You've done it again. This isn't the way to town!'

Tom's mum smiled into the car mirror. 'Oh, this is the way all right!' she said. They were driving through a maze of parking spaces and fences.

'Er . . . it really isn't, mum,' said Tom. 'This is just like the time you nearly drove us to Wales by accident when we were going to the supermarket!'

'That was an easy mistake to make!' frowned his mum. 'It's just around this corner anyway.'

Tom's gran turned round in her seat and gave her grandson a wink. 'You know, your mum and I are hitting the shops today,' she said with a smile.

'Yes,' grumbled Tom under his breath.

'But you aren't coming with us!' she cried. 'We're dropping you off just over here!'

'But . . .' Tom said, puzzled. 'What am I going to . . . WOW!'

The car rounded a final corner and came to a stop – *right in front of The David Beckham Academy*!

'You don't mean . . . am I going . . .?' Tom couldn't get his words out fast enough.

'Yes!' cried Tom's mum. 'You're going to spend three whole days in there, playing football until it comes out of your ears!'

'My treat!' said his gran. 'It's an early birthday present!'

Tom gasped and fumbled with the car door handle. 'You mean I'm going to . . .' The door burst open and he tumbled out head first, landing in a heap on the concrete. He looked up at the big glass doorway and turned back to the car with his mouth gaping.

'This is the best present *ever!*' he gasped. His gran leaned out of the car window and gave him a gentle push.

'Well, go on then,' she said. 'They'll be starting in a minute.'

Tom turned round and bounded towards the door. This was going to be *way* better than looking at hats!

BOOTING UP

Tom sat down on the changing-room bench and pulled the blue David Beckham Academy top he'd just been given over his head.

'Mffmfmmfmff!' he mumbled, struggling to find the arm holes.

'Eh?' said a tall, blond boy next to him. 'I'm James. Are you on my team? I think I noticed you when we were being divided into countries by the head coach!'

'Mfiffififfffff!' grunted Tom, trying to wriggle his head out. James grabbed

Tom's shirt and pulled it down for him.

'Phew, cheers,' said Tom, smoothing his hair down. 'Are you in team France too?'

'Yes. I reckon we've got a good chance as well. That lot over there are Spain and they don't look that good,' said James, pointing to the other side of the changing room. A group of smaller boys were putting their kits on and nervously looking round the crowded room.

'Yeah, Holland look a bit scary though!' said another of Tom's teammates, looking at some tough-looking boys already talking tactics in the corner. 'I don't fancy facing them in the tournament much!'

Looking around, Tom now realised that the Academy students had all grouped together into the teams picked by the head coach, Frank Evans. Teams that were named after some of the world's best footballing nations.

'Hey, nothing to worry about. I'm top scorer in our school league!' said Tom. 'Does anyone mind if I play up front?'

'I guess that's up to our coach!' said James.

Tom squeezed his feet into his tatty boots and fixed the sticky tape on the heel. 'Have any of you seen the new Predator boots?' he asked.

'*Have* I?' cried James. 'They look amazing! My mum won't let me have a pair though. Says I'm growing too fast at the moment and they won't last . . .'

Tom nodded. 'Mine too. I'll just have to become a professional footballer and buy my own, I suppose!'

James laughed. 'Yeah. I told my mum

I'd buy her a house when I'm playing for England!'

As all of the children filed out of the changing room another door flew open and a tall woman in a football kit bounded through it.

'Bonjour!' she cried. 'Which of you lot are France?'

Tom, James and a few other boys put their hands up.

'Then come with me. I'm Kelly, and I'll be your coach for the next three days!'

As the boys followed Kelly on to the pitch, James frowned. 'A lady coach, eh?' he said. 'I hope she's good!'

Tom turned round and was about to answer when something tall and bony crashed into him and left him sprawling on the floor like an upside-down woodlouse.

'Ooof!' he cried, untangling himself. 'Watch where you're going! You could have hurt me!'

A girl slightly taller than Tom stood up and dusted herself down. She had red curly hair pulled back in a tight ponytail, and was wearing a shiny new David Beckham Academy kit too. 'Watch out yourself,' she said. 'I nearly sprained my ankle!'

'Oh, yeah?' said Tom, drawing himself up an extra couple of centimetres. 'Well, I nearly twisted my knee!'

The girl was about to retaliate when Kelly turned round and stood between them.

'Hey, hey!' she said. 'Less arguing! Especially as you're going to be teammates. Boys – meet the final member of the France team. This is Kate!'

Tom looked up at Kelly in shock. 'You don't mean that we've got a *girl* on our team, do you?' he cried, staring at Kate. 'Now we've got no chance of winning the tournament. I hope you're ready to warm up the subs bench, Kate.'

'Tom, I've warned you once already,' said Kelly. 'How do you know Kate isn't better than you lot at football?'

'Because she's a girl!' said Tom, moodily.

James nudged Tom in the ribs. 'Actually, my sister's pretty good at footy, mate,' he said.

Kelly frowned. 'And *I'm* a girl, and I play for the England women's football team. Are you saying I'm no good at football either?'

'Well, no, that's different,' muttered Tom, looking at his feet. 'At least you've played lots of football. She's probably never even . . . even . . .'

Tom didn't finish his sentence. All the other boys were silently staring at Kate, their jaws hanging wide open. She was crouched on the floor beside them, lacing up her football boots; *a brand new pair of Predator boots.*

'Wow!' gasped James. 'Cool boots!'

Kate jumped up and gave Tom an angry look. 'What were you saying?' she said. 'I've probably never *what*?'

Tom stuttered with shock. 'Just because you've got nice boots, doesn't make you a good footballer,' he said.

Kate just raised her eyebrows and looked down at Tom's feet. The sticky

tape was peeling off his right boot.

'Yeah, well . . .' Tom began, but he couldn't think of anything else to say. He was still trying to think of a brilliant insult when Kate wandered off and began some professional-looking warm-up exercises at the side of the pitch.

'Nice comeback there, mate!' laughed James.

'Whatever. We'll see who's got what it takes on the pitch,' grumbled Tom. He plastered the tape on his heel as tight as possible and fumed silently.

'I don't care what boots she's wearing!' he muttered to James as the pair ran on to the pitch. 'She's still a girl!'

PITCH BATTLE

Tom stood on the centre spot, his foot trapping the ball in place. He tried to ignore the smiles on the faces of the opposing team, Brazil.

Tom could see that they expected to win this game, and he just hoped that he could prove them wrong – even with a girl on his side. Just then, Kate jogged over to the centre circle and stood opposite him.

'What do you think you're doing?' cried Tom. 'You're not taking the kick-off with me. Just get back in defence and try not to lose us the match.'

Kate frowned and tightened her ponytail. 'I've got a better idea,' she said. 'How about you stop complaining and let me help us to score some goals?'

Kelly was striding out to referee the game, the whistle already clamped between her teeth.

'Look, just go away,' growled Tom. 'This isn't a kickabout in the park, it's the first game of the tournament. And you are *not* taking the kick-off!'

But Kelly's whistle blew and, before Tom could say another word, Kate rolled the ball to him and jogged off to the wing.

'You –, you –' Tom fumed, as a Brazil player charged towards him. 'I wasn't even ready!'

As Tom hesitated, the Brazil player clattered into him before sprinting off with the ball. Kate hadn't just taken the kick-off; she'd made him look stupid too.

'Oi!' he yelled, jumping to his feet. 'Someone win the ball back!'

The Brazil player rounded James easily and was squaring up for a shot on goal when, to Tom's surprise, Kate slid in with a perfect last-second tackle and won the ball.

'Good challenge, Kate!' shouted Kelly.

Kate was off and running up the pitch looking to set up a France attack. She dragged the ball sideways, sending a Brazil player the wrong way, then laid the ball neatly off to Tom. He turned on his heel and set off down the pitch at a sprint. The Brazil defenders moved across their area to

block him. He dropped his shoulder and rounded one player, but they had half their team back by now and he found himself surrounded by Brazil defenders.

'Someone help him out!' cried James from further down the pitch.

Tom shielded the ball with his body and held off the nearest defender. He looked up for someone to pass to. In an instant, Kate was behind him on the touchline.

'Tom! Knock it back!' she cried.

Tom scowled. The Brazil defenders were snapping at his heels, but there was *no way* he was passing it to her! He shoulder-barged the player next to him out of the way and tried to bundle through the crowd of defenders to the goal, but a long leg scooped the ball out from under his feet and he ended up sprawled on the floor in a heap.

'Why didn't you pass to me?' shouted Kate, as Brazil streamed down the pitch on the break. 'I could have scored from there.'

Tom was still dusting himself down when Kate broke into a sprint and stole the ball back from the Brazil striker who was dribbling it down the pitch. She controlled the ball, looked up to check her options, then played the ball sideways to James.

James knocked the ball back to her in a neat one-two. 'Now get up there,' he encouraged. Kate set off down the wing.

She dribbled round two players easily, before sliding the ball through a third pair of legs and dashing round him to collect it. She trapped the ball under her foot, glanced up at Tom, then sent a long pass in his direction, over towards the penalty area. It split the defence perfectly, landing at his feet.

'Wow! Great pass!' cried James. Several other players were watching with their hands on their hips, impressed at Kate's skill, forgetting for a moment that they were playing too.

Tom controlled the ball neatly, then swivelled round fast, sent the goalkeeper the wrong way with a step-over and blasted the ball past him into the net.

'Goooaaaaalllll!' he roared, charging down the pitch with his hands in the air.

Kate ran over with her hand raised for a high five. 'Nice finish,' she smiled.

But Tom dodged around her, kept running, and dived into the mass of celebrating France players further down the pitch.

'Great goal, mate!' said James, patting him on the back.

Kate, however, didn't seem so happy. She strode up to Tom and gave him a jab with her elbow. 'You weren't the only one involved in that goal,' she muttered.

'I don't need you to help me score,' Tom answered back as the game restarted.

He leaped into action, tackling a Brazil player. He won the ball and set back off down the pitch with it at full pelt. Kate sprinted ahead of him past the Brazil defence.

'Over here!' she yelled. 'You'd better pass to me this time!'

Tom looked up. Kate was in a great goal-scoring position. He was about to chip the ball through to her, but hesitated at the last minute. Did he really want that annoying girl to get a goal? Instead, he drew his foot back and blasted a long-range shot wide of the post. Several team members tutted behind him.

Kate wasn't just disappointed with his shot; she was furious!

'Why won't you pass to me?' she howled, stamping her foot and going red in the face. 'We'd be three–nil up if it weren't for you!'

'If it weren't for *me*?' protested Tom. 'I'm the one who scored our goal. This is supposed to be a serious football team,' he carried on, his voice getting louder and higher every minute. 'We should win the tournament! And it's all going to go wrong because we've got *you* on our side!'

Tom paused for breath with his hands on his hips. As he panted, he slowly became aware that everyone on the pitch was staring at him in silence. James caught his eye then quickly looked away again.

'Er . . .' he mumbled. Kelly strode up with a black look on her face.

'Tom Walsh!' she said angrily. 'Leave the pitch right *now*! You're substituted. This is *not* your football team, and you won't be playing in it again until you learn a better team attitude!'

Tom gasped, opened and closed his mouth, then stomped off the pitch. He watched from the bench as Kate made a series of brilliant tackles and passes in midfield.

'This is *so* not what I had planned for my first day at The Academy!' he muttered under his breath as the whole team congratulated Kate after the game.

TACTICAL BLUNDER

The following day, James plonked himself down at a desk next to Tom at the front of one of the Academy classrooms.

'You're sulking about Kate, aren't you?' sighed James, noticing Tom's scowl.

'No,' growled Tom. 'I'm . . . thinking!'

'Yeah. Thinking about the massive sulk you're in because you were substituted yesterday,' laughed James.

'Well, it's not fair,' said Tom. 'We shouldn't have a girl as the star player on our team!'

'I don't see why not, when she's as good as she is,' said James. 'She's got a right foot like . . .' He was about to launch into a lengthy description of Kate's passing skills when he noticed Tom's scowl getting even deeper.

'Well, anyway, if you want to even things up, why not show her how smart you are in this tactics session?' said James, dropping his voice to a whisper as the classroom filled up and Kelly arrived.

'You're right!' Tom replied, as Kelly pressed a button and a diagram of a football pitch appeared on the whiteboard at the front. 'I bet Kate's tactical knowledge is useless. Girls hate that kind of stuff.'

'Now, we're going to talk about tactics in different situations,' began Kelly.

Twenty-two dots appeared on the whiteboard, representing the players on each team. 'Team A is one–nil down. This defender has the ball. What should he do now to get them back in the game?'

Tom's hand rocketed up before she'd even finished the sentence.

'He should chip a long ball up to the star striker, Kelly!' he cried. 'He can blast the ball in from outside the box, and it'll be one–all!'

Kelly smiled. 'That's certainly *one* way to do it,' she said. 'But how about more of a team effort? Yes, Kate!'

Kate had her hand up too. 'The defender could pass to a midfielder, who could cross the ball to the striker once the opposition's defence have pushed out. By drawing players out of position, the midfielder

creates space for the striker to nip behind them and score.'

'Great answer, well done!' said Kelly. 'Can everyone see what a good strategy this is?'

Everyone nodded, except for Tom. He was glaring at Kate.

'What about this situation?' Kelly continued. 'Team A's striker has the ball on the edge of the area, but he's surrounded by defenders. What ball should he play?'

'That happened yesterday,' hissed Kate under her breath. 'But *someone* over there hogged the ball and I missed a chance to score.'

Tom turned bright red with anger and put his hand up to answer.

'The striker could dribble round the defenders and score again,' he said. 'He certainly shouldn't pass to a spoiled midfielder with fancy boots!' he added to James, under his breath.

Kelly frowned. 'It's not all about star strikers, Tom!' she said. 'The striker here has a whole team to help him.'

Kate had her hand up again. 'He could shield the ball with his body until a midfielder comes up and helps him. Then he could pass to him – *or her* – and they could link up with the rest of the team to get around the defence.'

As she said the word 'her', she narrowed her eyes and glared at Tom.

'Good answer again, Kate,' said Kelly. 'You know your tactics.'

Tom was getting more cross by the minute. Was this girl going to make him feel stupid *every day* at The Academy?

'But why bother with all that stuff if you've got a good striker on the pitch?' he blurted out. 'Why not just give the ball to him so he can score?'

Kelly frowned again. 'Because one player on their own can't do half as much as a team playing together can,' she explained patiently. 'A good striker may get two goals in a match. But a good striker with a good midfielder behind them, and a good defence, will create more chances and let in fewer goals. Remember, it's all about the build-up play when the opposition have an organised defence.'

'Humph!' muttered Tom under his breath. 'I still think my way is easier!'

'Anyway,' said Kelly, switching the whiteboard off. 'Thanks to Kate's excellent answers, I'm awarding the team top marks for this tactics session. Now, let's get back on the pitch!'

Everyone cheered and, as they filed out of the classroom excitedly, the boys were falling over each other to pat Kate on the back.

'Good one, Kate!'

'That was brilliant! We could win the tournament!'

'Well done,' said James before Tom scowled at him.

'I've had enough of this!' hissed Tom. 'She's *not* going to spoil my time at The Academy!'

As the other players jogged out on to the pitch, Tom grabbed Kate's arm. 'Can I have a word?' he said, leading her off down a corridor.

'Sure!' said Kate smugly. 'Perhaps I could give you a lesson in football tactics.'

'I'm warning you . . .' said Tom.

'Warning me about what? Are you going to have another tantrum? Or . . .'

Kate stopped mid-sentence as Tom gave her a push through an open door. She found herself stumbling backwards into the disabled toilet.

'Hey!' shouted Kate. 'Stop pushi—'

Tom shut the door behind her and looked around for something to wedge under the handle.

'Oi! Let me out!' cried Kate from behind the door. 'You're just jealous cos a girl is better at football than you!'

'I am *not*!' cried Tom, grabbing a chair with his free hand. 'And you *aren't* better than me!'

He jammed the chair's back under the door handle and stepped away. Kate's muffled cries could just be heard.

'I'd like to see your Predator boots get you out of *that* one!' he said, before jogging out towards the pitch.

This time *he* was going to be the star player!

LONE STRIKER

As Tom jogged out on to the pitch, the rest of the team was standing around waiting to kick off.

'You took your time,' complained James. 'And where's Kate?'

Tom shrugged. 'I, er . . . saw her limping to the physio room a minute ago,' he said, trying to sound innocent. 'I think she sprained her ankle.'

James frowned. 'Sprained her ankle? In the classroom?'

Tom shrugged again. 'Look, what do I

know? We'll just have to start without her.'

'Well, I hope you're ready to score some goals then,' James replied as they kicked off. 'You'll have to be the main man if Kate's injured.'

Tom smiled to himself and jogged into the opposition penalty area. That's exactly what he had in mind.

'Over here!' he cried, dodging the boy who was marking him and running into space. 'I'm free!'

But instead of sending a neat pass through the defence, the France midfielder stumbled over the ball and lost possession instead. Tom tutted to himself.

'Come on, France!' he yelled as the midfield struggled to win the ball back. 'We can do better than this.'

Things didn't improve as the match

went on, however. There was no doubt about it – the midfield was struggling. The players weren't winning tackles, and weren't even getting *near* their opponents half the time.

Finally, James charged out of defence, won the ball, and rolled it off to a midfield player. France streamed down the pitch on the attack – Tom leading the way by charging through Brazil's defence.

'Over the top!' he cried, jostling with a defender. 'That's it!'

A France midfielder was running up the centre of the pitch with the ball. He glanced up at Tom, drew his foot back, and launched the ball forwards. Instead of dipping into the Brazil penalty area for Tom to run on to, though, it just kept on rising. The ball soared over Tom's head, over the

Brazil goal, and bounced off the referee's head on the next pitch.

Tom groaned. 'I said over the top, not launch it into space!' he grumbled as the Brazil goalkeeper set off to retrieve the ball. 'Can't anyone back there pass?'

His teammates just glared back at him.

As the match went on, Tom's frustration grew and grew. He seemed to be spending the whole match standing on his own on the edge of the area, without getting so much as a sniff of the ball. Not one person in France's midfield seemed able to get a decent pass to him. As he stood with his hands on his hips next to a Brazil defender, another hopeless pass sailed over his head and bounced off the roof.

'This is ridiculous!' he cried. 'You lot are *useless*!'

His teammates scowled back at him. 'It's all right for you, standing around in the penalty area,' said one of them – a tall, thin boy with messy hair called Sam. 'How about coming back here and winning the ball?'

Tom yelled back. 'Because I'm the striker! You're supposed to *look out*!'

While the two argued, their opponents had surged through the midfield and were bearing down on goal. James lunged at the attacker with a desperate sliding tackle, but he was too late. The striker looked up, dodged James's outstretched foot, then slid a perfect shot past the keeper and into the France net.

'No!' cried Tom as their opponents celebrated wildly. 'This is *terrible!*'

As the half-time whistle blew, he stormed off the pitch and beckoned the rest of the team over to the bench.

'What's the matter with you lot?' he fumed at his teammates. 'I might as well be playing with my gran for all the decent passes I've got! And now you go and let in a soft goal like that!'

The team members started grumbling amongst themselves. 'Well, it's not like you've done much to help out, is it?' moaned

Sam. 'You've hardly touched the ball.'

Tom went bright red with annoyance. 'That's my point! You're supposed to be passing me the ball, but you're *useless*!'

'Well, if you're so great, why don't you come and *get* the ball?' grunted Sam. 'And anyway, who made *you* captain?'

Tom was about to reply when Kelly strode over and intervened.

'Hey, hey!' she cried. 'How about a bit of teamwork here? Why don't you start planning the second half?'

Tom and the rest of the team looked sheepishly at their feet. Tom sat down on the bench and frowned: with Kate out of the way, *he* was meant to be the star player. But it wasn't going according to plan.

His daydream was disturbed by a rough, gravelly voice behind his left ear.

'You know what you need?' it said.

Tom turned round to see a short, wrinkly old man standing just behind him.

'What do I need?' said Tom. 'And how would you know anyway?' he added.

'You need that girl back in the team,' said the old man. 'And I'd know because I was a groundsman for forty years at Manchester United, and now I work here at The Academy. I've seen all the great strikers training.'

Tom raised his eyebrows. 'And what's that got to do with Kate?' he said.

The old man took off his cap and scratched his head. 'Because every striker I've ever seen needed a good midfielder behind them. That's why David Beckham is such a great player. He makes any striker he plays with ten times better!'

Tom fiddled with his shin pads uncomfortably. 'Yeah, well, Kate's hardly David Beckham, is she?' he mumbled.

'She's got a great right foot on her! And she can pass the ball better than any eleven-year-old I've seen in the last few years. Believe me, lad!' The groundsman smiled, strolling off with his broom. 'That's what you need! That girl back in the team!'

Tom was about to shout something after him when a movement across the pitch caught his eye.

A very red-faced Kate was striding through the door and heading straight for him.

RUNNING SCARED

Tom shuddered and tried his best to look innocent. How could he possibly have thought he could get away with this?

'Are you all right?' Kelly asked her. 'How's your sore ankle?'

'It's fine,' replied Kate, still not taking her eyes off Tom. 'Never better.'

Tom looked at his tatty boots. This was going to be bad. Kate was going to tell Kelly what he'd done and he would be thrown out of The Academy.

The rest of the team just looked

relieved to have her back.

Tom shuddered. He pictured his mum's angriest face, then multiplied it by a thousand. She and his gran must have saved for *ages* to send him here and now he was going to be booted out!

'Kate?' said Kelly. 'Is there something you want to tell me? You look upset.'

Tom began to get to his feet, heading towards the changing room. There was no point in dragging this out.

'Might as well get this over with!' he said under his breath. He was furious with himself for being so stupid. And all because he was jealous of a girl.

'No, I just want to get on with the rest of the game,' Kate said.

He couldn't meet her gaze, looking at his feet instead. He was bewildered; why hadn't Kate told on him?

'Well, we'd better get on with the match!' said Kelly after a moment.

Tom was still frozen in shock. Did this mean he was off the hook? But why would Kate help him out? She must hate him! He was still standing gawping when Kate jogged past him on to the pitch.

'Th-th-thanks!' said Tom, as she ran towards him. But Kate just muttered, 'Don't think I've forgiven you, Tom. If that chair hadn't fallen over I'd still be in there.'

Tom couldn't think of anything to say. His jaw was hanging open.

'You OK, mate?' said James, trotting over. 'You look terrified!'

Tom snapped out of his trance. 'No, I'm, er . . . I'm fine! Just a bit surprised.'

'It's Kate, isn't it?' chuckled James. 'She gave you a proper evil look there.'

Tom jogged up to the centre circle. 'Nah, she's OK,' he said.

'Well, I'm glad she's back, anyhow!' James laughed. 'Now you might actually get some proper service in the penalty area. Is there any chance you two'll stop arguing and actually pass to each other this half?'

Tom looked over at Kate, who still had a furious look on her face. 'Er . . . I'll give it a go,' he said to James nervously.

'Now, let's win this match!' he exclaimed, plonking the ball down on the centre spot and looking up at Kelly.

'Hang on a minute, team! Don't kick off yet!' she cried. 'Kate, can I have a quick word?'

Kate nodded and jogged over to the touchline where the coach was standing.

'Kate, I know you're still having problems with one of your teammates,' said Kelly. 'But I'm not going to push it any further. It's down to the two of you to sort things out.'

Kate nodded, but didn't say anything.

'However, I will give you a piece of advice,' Kelly continued. 'It's written in

massive letters in the hallway of The Academy and is one of David Beckham's favourite sayings: Stay Focused.'

Kate nodded again.

'I've lost count of the number of times boys have told me I shouldn't play football,' sighed Kelly. 'But I kept on going, and now I play for the England women's team. So just ignore them when they're being mean, and get out there and show them all how good you are on the pitch. It's the only way to beat the bullies!'

Kate still didn't say anything, but she cast her eyes over to the ball on the centre circle.

'Remember – forget about the boys, and concentrate on the game,' said Kelly, patting Kate on the back. 'Now, get out there and play!'

Kate ran back to the centre circle where Tom was standing and turned to face the team.

'Come on, you lot!' she yelled. 'We can still win this!'

The team cheered. Everyone seemed relieved that Kate was back in midfield.

'Oi! Hang on . . .' Tom began, but didn't finish his sentence. He was about to complain about Kate taking the kick-off, but realised he wasn't really in a position to start moaning.

'Here you go,' he said, dropping the ball at her feet.

Kate trapped it with her right foot and gave him a glare. 'You'd better get up there and start scoring, or I'll be doing it for you!'

Tom gulped.

'Right,' he said, and the second half kicked off.

GOAL FEST

Tom ducked behind his marker and sprinted into the penalty area for the twentieth time that day. This time, however, there was a difference: the ball floated over the defenders' heads and landed neatly at his feet.

'Good ball, Kate!' yelled James from behind.

Tom rounded the last defender, but the angle was too tight: he couldn't squeeze the ball past the keeper. He side-footed it through the goalie's legs, but it bounced off the post and rolled over the line for a goal kick.

'Yeah, nice pass!' he said to Kate as they jogged back down the pitch. Kate ignored him and turned the other way.

'Come on, France!' yelled James as the keeper placed the ball down for his goal kick. 'We've got our star midfielder back. We can still win this!'

Tom had to admit that the team was transformed now that Kate was back. Instead of dawdling on the edge of the area watching terrible passes sail over his head, he was constantly receiving the ball in good goal-scoring positions. The old groundsman was right – a good midfielder *did* make you a better striker.

'Make a run!' cried Kate, waking Tom from his thoughts. She had won the ball straight from the goal kick and was tearing down the right wing. Tom sprang into action. He darted into the middle of the pitch, pretended to go left, then sprinted right to throw off the Brazil defender in front of him. He found himself in space in the Brazil penalty area.

Kate saw his run out of the corner of her eye. She held off the Brazil left back

with her shoulder and chipped a pass towards goal. It landed perfectly halfway between the sprinting Tom and the advancing Brazil goalkeeper.

'Shoot!' yelled Kate as he reached the ball. But Tom controlled it and dribbled across the area, taking the ball neatly away from the keeper. As four defenders charged towards him, desperately trying to tackle him, Tom calmly rolled the ball into the back of the empty net.

'Yesss!' he roared, sprinting down the pitch with both arms in the air.

'Woo-hooo!' cried James.

Tom ran up to Kate, his hand raised for a high five. 'Great pass,' he said. But Kate turned on her heel, leaving him with his hand in the air like an idiot.

'Just because I didn't tell on you, doesn't

mean I've let you off!' she hissed at Tom. 'You locked me in the loo, remember!'

'Yeah, erm . . . sorry about that,' said Tom. 'I was . . .'

'Oh, just get on with the game!' said Kate, before speeding off to floor the opposition forward with a perfect sliding tackle. Tom set off at full speed. He overlapped Kate on the right wing and she sent a long pass over the top for him to run on to.

Tom collected the ball with his right foot and looked up, but his path was blocked by the big Brazil left back. He trapped the ball and held the defender off with his back, struggling to shield the ball from the boy's long legs. Kate spotted he was in trouble and darted up behind him.

'Knock it back!' she yelled. Tom rolled

the ball over to her. 'Now get in the box!'
she cried.

Tom sprinted towards the goal, easily
outrunning the big left back. Once
again, Kate sent a perfect pass through the
defence to his feet. He darted past the last
defender and hit the ball first time,
powering it towards the top-right corner
with all his might.

The opposition defence froze and
couldn't take their eyes off the ball,
watching in slow motion as it flew
towards the goal. Their keeper charged
across his line and launched himself into
the air, aiming a flailing hand at the ball as
he jumped. He just managed to get a
fingertip to it before crashing to the ground,
sending the ball millimetres wide of
the post.

'Yesss!' panted the goalkeeper, picking himself up.

'Corner,' announced Kelly, blowing her whistle. 'Hurry up and take it – there's only a minute left on the clock!'

Kate picked the ball up and carefully placed it next to the corner flag. Team France piled into the Brazil penalty area, desperate to get a last-minute winner. Even France's goalie ran down the pitch to stand on the edge of the box.

Tom looked over at Kate and jostled for a position in the box.

Far post, Kate mouthed slowly at him. Tom nodded. He jostled for a moment longer then, as Kate booted the ball high across the face of the goal, he darted backwards to the back post. The defender next to him was too late to follow, and

Tom leaped into the air as high as he could. The ball dipped perfectly at the last minute, and he powered the ball towards the goal with his forehead.

'Yesss!' Tom roared, collapsing back on to the pitch in a tangle of legs and arms. He could see the ball bouncing in the back of the net, past the arms of the helpless goalkeeper.

'Yeeeaaahhhh!' cried James, piling on top of Tom. Within seconds, he was buried under a sea of France players, all cheering and congratulating him.

'We did it!' yelled James.

'Mngfmgfn!' gasped Tom, unable to breathe under the bundle of celebrating players.

He wriggled free and looked about the pitch. The only player not celebrating was

Kate. She was walking off the pitch.

'Great corner, Kate!' cried Tom.

But Kate didn't look round.

STAY FOCUSED

The next day, Team France trotted off the pitch at the end of their last match, grinning from ear to ear. James gave Kate a friendly slap on the back.

'Well done!' he panted. 'We'd never have won the tournament without you! Or you either, Tom — that hat-trick in the final was awesome!'

'Cheers, mate!' said Tom. 'I just can't believe we won!'

'Do you think David Beckham will be dishing the medals out?' asked James, hopping from foot to foot.

'I think it's very unlikely!' said Tom. 'He was on TV playing abroad last night.'

'Clever clogs,' muttered James.

'Still, it's the trophy that counts!' said Tom, punching the air.

'I thought it was the taking part that counts?' asked James.

'Yeah, taking part in winning the tournament – like we just did!' laughed Tom.

'Right, are you lot ready?' said Kelly, wandering over to the team members still gathered at the edge of the pitch after their final game. 'It's nearly medal time. And David's mum is here to hand them out!'

'Cool!' said James. 'So we *do* get to meet a Beckham after all!'

'I wonder if she's like normal mums?' said James.

'Like, does she still tell David off if he walks his muddy football boots over the carpet?' laughed Tom. 'Why don't you ask her when you go up for your medal?'

'Speaking of which,' said James as the team gathered together, 'who's going up to get the trophy for the team?'

Everyone instantly looked at Tom. He had scored 14 goals in the tournament after all, including the hat-trick in the final.

'Tom,' said James. 'You *are* our top scorer.'

Tom was wondering how to accept without seeming arrogant, when a voice at the back piped up.

'Hey! What about Kate? We were

rubbish without her on the team!' said Sam.

'True,' said James. 'What does everyone else think?'

'She set up all our goals! She should definitely do it!' shouted Sam, giving Tom an evil look. He still hadn't forgotten how Tom had shouted at him during their terrible first half without Kate.

Kate herself was standing slightly away from the rest of the team, as usual. She was taking off her Predator boots and putting them in her special boot bag.

'Kate, tell them you want to go and get the trophy,' said Sam. 'It won't be fair otherwise.'

Kate sighed. 'I don't suppose anything I say is going to stop Tom from going up there and getting it,' she muttered.

While the team was still arguing about who to send up, Kelly strode over and led them to a crowd of other children waiting for the ceremony to begin.

'Have you chosen who's going up to meet Mrs Beckham?' she asked as Team France sat down at the front.

'Yes,' said Tom. 'We have.'

Kelly waited.

'And?' she said. 'Who is it?'

Tom thought for a moment and looked at the team. 'It's Kate!' Everyone gasped. Even Sam was speechless.

'Really?' said Kate, as amazed as everyone else.

'Sure!' said Tom. 'Sam's right – we were useless without you on the team. We wouldn't have won without you.'

For the first time since they met,

Kate smiled at Tom.

'Plus, it's the least I could do after I . . . well, after you-know-what!' he whispered to her, while the others chatted excitedly.

'Wow! Thanks!' said Kate, and followed Kelly up to the prize platform. Mrs Beckham was waiting in the middle with a trophy and a big medal. She hung the medal around Kate's neck, pressed the trophy into her hand, and the crowd erupted in applause. Kate held the trophy in the air and grinned at the cheering faces.

'Well done!' said Mrs Beckham, standing next to her. 'I'm delighted to see such a talented girl doing well at The Academy – and becoming so popular.'

Kate laughed. 'I suppose you're right!' she said.

'Well, my David has a favourite phrase.

He always says Stay Focused, no matter what!' said Mrs Beckham.

Kate smiled. 'Yes, I'm sure I've heard that somewhere before!' She bounded off the stage where Tom was waiting with his hand in the air for a high five. This time, Kate didn't leave him hanging.

Ten minutes later, he was sitting cross-legged by the car and taking his boots and shin pads off. Tom's mum tried to squeeze a word in edgeways as Tom told her all about how great The Academy was.

'And the pitches are huge,' he said. 'And covered by these giant arches. It's dead exciting to play on them!'

He peeled the tape from his boots, slid them off his feet and chucked them into the car boot.

'And we won the tournament! I scored fourteen goals. And I made a friend called James. And then . . .'

He was about to put his trainers on when something black and heavy fell from the sky into his lap.

'Ooof!' he said, picking it up. 'What the . . .'

It was a shiny, nearly new pair of Predator

boots. Tom looked up to see where they'd come from.

'Kate!' he said, jumping to his feet.

'My mum bought me a new pair for winning the tournament,' said Kate, 'and I remembered I knew someone who could do with a decent pair of boots. I hope they fit!'

Tom grinned and turned the Predator

boots over in his hands.

'Wow! Thanks a million! They're amazing!'

Kate turned to run back to her mum's car, which was parked nearby.

'Kate!' shouted Tom.

'What?' she cried, pausing for a moment.

'I was wrong,' he cried. 'You do deserve boots like these!'

Kate smiled and ducked into her car.

'Who was that?' asked Tom's mum, bundling him into the back seat before he could start taking about The Academy again.

'She was our star midfielder!' said Tom as they drove away. 'Almost as good as David Beckham himself!'

TURN THE PAGE TO READ A SNEAK PREVIEW OF THE FIFTH BOOK IN THE DAVID BECKHAM ACADEMY SERIES!

GOING DUTCH

George polished his glasses and put them back on.

'I don't get it. If we're Holland, why don't we get orange kits?'

Ben sighed as he pulled the blue David Beckham Academy football shirt over his head.

'Look, we're not *really* Holland,' he explained for the second time. 'That's just a name for our team. That lot over there are France. And I know they're not French because three of them go to my school!'

'So we aren't going to have a Dutch coach then?' George asked.

'No,' said Ben patiently. 'We'll have an English coach. We're just *called* Holland.'

George seemed to get the message at last and bent down to lace up his football boots. 'Well, I don't see why they have to make it so confusing!' he muttered.

Ben was about to suggest that it was actually quite simple when three more boys shoved their way through the mass of bodies in the changing room.

'Are you lot Holland?' asked a tall boy with scruffy brown hair.

'Yep!' nodded Ben. 'Welcome to the team! I'm Ben and this is George.'

The team members quickly introduced themselves and pulled on their new football kits.

'So who's your favourite player?' asked George, smoothing down his ginger hair in a nearby mirror.

'David Beckham, of course!' said Ben. 'What about you?'

Within minutes, all the members of the Holland team were arguing about their favourite players and boasting about how they were *definitely* going to be the best team at The Academy.

'I'm telling you guys, we *have* to win!' cried Ben.

'Yeah!' cried George. 'How about we pick our positions before the coach gets here? I play on the left wing!'

'I'm a midfielder,' said Ben.

'I play in midfield too!' said another boy.

'What about you?' said George, to a

short boy with dark hair who had just joined the group. 'What's your favourite position?'

The boy looked blankly at George and didn't answer.

'Hey!' said Ben, assuming the boy hadn't heard. 'You're in Holland, right? What's your name?'

The boy looked blank again and shrugged nervously.

'You must know your name!' said Ben. 'What are you called?'

The boy's face suddenly lit up. 'Stefan!' he said in a foreign accent.

'Aha!' said George. 'I knew it! A Dutchman!'

Ben rolled his eyes. 'Will you shut up about Dutchmen? I've told you . . .'

But George was questioning Stefan in a slow, loud voice.

'Are . . . you . . . from . . . Holland?' he asked, mouthing the words as he spoke. Stefan just shrugged again.

'Do . . . you . . . speak . . . English?' George continued.

Stefan seemed to understand and shook his head. 'No English,' he said.

George looked smugly at Ben. 'See!' he said. 'He's not English. He's *definitely* from Holland!'

Ben groaned. 'Just because he's foreign, doesn't mean he's Dutch!' he replied with a sigh. 'He doesn't even have a Dutch accent!'

Stefan seemed to realise they were talking about him and started to blush. He began fidgeting with a pile of football stickers in his shorts pocket . . .

TO BE CONTINUED

Collect all the books in
The David Beckham Academy range

STORYBOOKS

Twin Trouble	ISBN 978 1 4052 4524 1	£4.99
Le Football	ISBN 978 1 4052 4525 8	£4.99
Save the Day	ISBN 978 1 4052 4526 5	£4.99
Bossy Boots	ISBN 978 1 4052 4527 2	£4.99

ACTIVITY BOOKS

How-to Handbook	ISBN 978 1 4052 4669 9	£4.99
Ultimate Football Sticker Book	ISBN 978 1 4052 4670 5	£4.99

ANNUAL

2010 Annual	ISBN 978 1 4052 4644 6	£7.99